# Be on the lookout...

Look for the dung beetle on each page for an added component of fun!

"Willlllll-soooooooon!!!" sang Mummy Wombat. "The sun is beginning to rise so it's time to get ready for bed!"

Wilson shuffled to his bedroom. "Mummy, I don't want to go to bed," he grumbled.

"Oh, why not?" Mummy asked.

"Well," Wilson explained, "thinking about going to bed makes my tummy feel wiggly."

**Did you know?**
Wombats are nocturnal marsupials that live in Australia. Nocturnal animals sleep during the day and stay up at night.

To my dreams-come-true, Abby, Caleb and Elizabeth, my once-little kids who are now incredible adults and have taught me the beauty of creation, laughter, and bedtime stories. To my husband Brian, always my biggest fan and greatest encourager. To my mom and dad who read me nighttime stories when I was little. Love you all!

- Amy S. Orlovich -

To all my sweet nieces and nephews, may you focus on the beauty in your lives and leave your worries behind.

- James Koenig -

For my kids, Clover and Jameson. Even though life has handed us plenty to worry about, your love has given me the confidence to persevere.

- Denise Arends -

## Instructions from the author:

The intention of this book is to help kids learn how to identify their feelings and cope when they are worried, especially at bedtime. Another aspect of this book is to help kids learn to recognize when they are feeling anxious, scared, or even peaceful and safe. It is important they learn to tune in and interpret the signals their body is giving them. I also introduce the "what-if-worries" which most of us have at some point. "What if this happens? What if that happens?" The "what-if-worries" can overwhelm and preoccupy our minds and that can be exhausting. We are all like Wilson sometimes!

Another component of this book is to learn scientific facts about the awesomely wonderful wombats! Some of the facts are sure to amaze even the most skeptical readers. You can't make this stuff up, so be sure to laugh when it's funny. There is additional information in the back of the book on the various animals mentioned throughout the book under the heading "Wombat Bed and Breakfast", as well as some pages to help parents, teachers, and caregivers navigate and understand more of the heart of teaching your kids to cope. I hope you love Wilson and his family and friends as much as I do.

May you all learn to battle the "what-if-worries" with your swords of "what-is-truth" and sleep peacefully in your safe beds tonight.

Sweet dreams,

- Amy

# Wilson the Wombat
## AND THE NIGHTTIME WHAT-IF WORRIES

**By:**

Amy S. Orlovich, Licensed Clinical Professional Counselor

**Illustrated By:**

James Koenig

Wilson the Wombat and The Nighttime What-If Worries

Written by Amy S. Orlovich, MA, LCPC, Illustrated by James Koenig, Coloring by Denise Arends

Mummy pulled Wilson up onto her tiny lap. She whispered into his furry little ear, "Sometimes a wiggly tummy means you're worried. And sometimes it means you have to go potty! So mosey down to the bathroom, go potty, and brush your teeth. Then we'll see how you are feeling."

**Did you know?**
Wombats are great at digging! They dig tunnels much larger and longer than they need to, which allows other small animals a living space or a temporary shelter to escape from harm.

**Did you also know?**
Many Australian animals may live in a wombat's burrow, including bilbies, blue-tongued skinks, dung beetles, echidnas, fairy penguins, rabbits, birds, and small rock wallabies!

Wilson padded down the dirt hallway to the bathroom where he brushed his

teeth, taking special care of his new front ones. Daddy called from the kitchen,

"Don't forget your molars! That's where you do all your important chewing!"

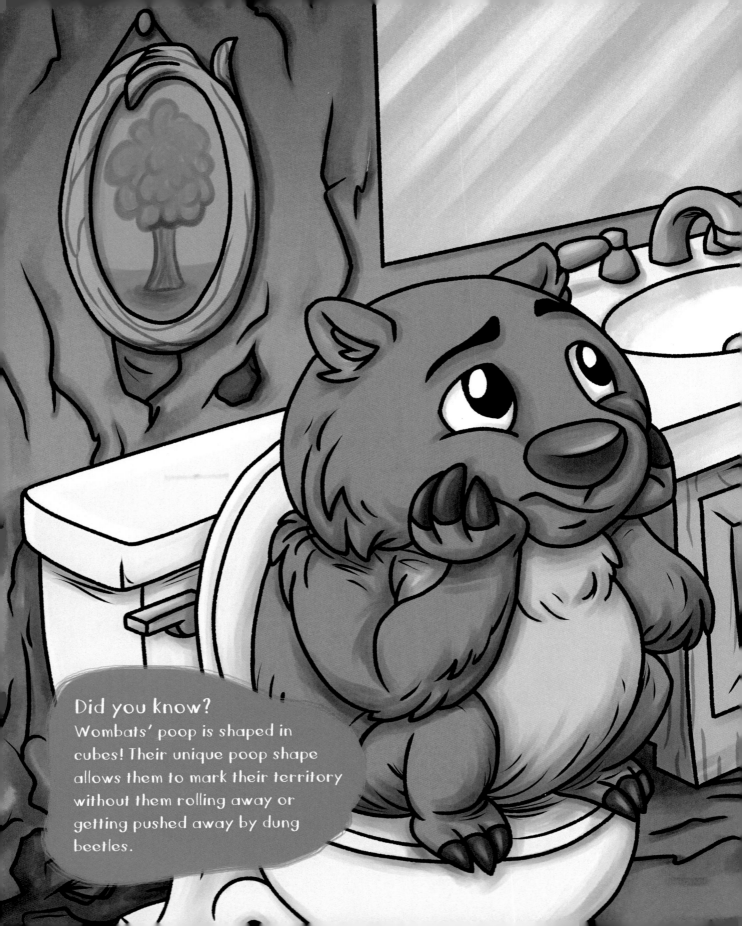

Did you know?
Wombats' poop is shaped in cubes! Their unique poop shape allows them to mark their territory without them rolling away or getting pushed away by dung beetles.

Then Wilson sat down on the toilet where he tinkled and even pooped a couple of cubes! He then washed his small, clawed hands very well with soap and water and went back to his room.

"How's your tummy now?" Mummy asked.

"Well... it is a little bit more gurgly now," replied Wilson. "Because what if... what if... What if something tries to come into our home?"

Mummy Wombat nodded her head in understanding and asked, "Wilson, do you think you have the what-if-worries?"

"Yes, I think I do!" he exclaimed.

### Did you know?
Mommy wombats have upside down shaped pouches on their tummy where their joey lives. This allows the mommy to dig out a new burrow or tunnel without filling up her pouch with dirt! And since wombats walk on all four legs, the joey won't fall out!

Mummy explained, "When the what-if-worries crowd our minds, remember to think about the what-IS-truths! The truth is Daddy and I both have extra big and very tough bottoms! We can use them to block the entrance to our home and if we need help, you will be there too!"

Wilson giggled, "Yes, that is true. We do have extra big and super tough rear ends that will keep us safe from anything coming in here!"

Did you know?
Wombats have very hard rumps. In fact, their rear ends are made of hard material called cartilage (like what your nose is made of). Wombats also have extra tough skin on their bottoms and very small tails. So when an intruder threatens the burrow, they plug the opening with their backside and the intruder can't get in!

"So how is your tummy now?" asked Daddy shaking his bootie in good fun.

"It is still wiggly and gurgly," Wilson quietly explained, "because, Daddy, what if my what-if-worried-mind won't stop worrying?"

"Let's talk about that." Daddy said. "How about we make a chart and write down three what-if-worries. Then, next to each, we will write the what-is-truths."

| What-if Worries | What-is Truths |
|---|---|
| What if something breaks in? | Daddy and Mummy's big booties! |
| What if I forget my spelling words? | My teacher will help me |
| What if I never sleep? | I will sleep great ☺ tomorrow. |

**Did you know?**
Everybody has "what-if worries," not only you! And it can be hard to turn off those worries at nighttime. You can try writing down or saying what you are worried about. An adult can help you find the truth about that worry or you may already know! Reminding yourself of truth breathes peace into your mind and body.

"All of us have what-if-worries sometimes. But it is important to remember that we cannot fight every worry we think of, because they have not happened yet!" Daddy explained.

Mummy agreed saying, "It is good to think through our worries, but thinking and thinking and thinking does not help! We become like weary warriors battling an invisible dragon with our sword of worries. And do you know what? Sometimes there isn't even a dragon at all, just empty air!"

Wilson was beginning to understand, "So sometimes I worry about things that won't even happen! That is silly. I shouldn't worry about things that aren't happening!"

### Did you know?
It is exhausting to worry about something that has not yet happened!
Those are the "what-if-worries" and you don't need to do it!
Instead remind yourself of what you KNOW to be true and remind your body that it is ok to feel safe when you are safe.

Wilson began to smile his big toothy grin, "So me lying here and thinking about all my what-if-worries just wears me out! And I don't need to do that! When a worry pops into my head, I will put away the sword of worries and I will battle it with my sword of truth. I can let my mind rest in the truth!"

**Did you know?**
Worries will pop into your head sometimes, especially when you do not want them to, and that is ok. Just notice the worry and imagine it floating away in a bubble or vanishing into thin air! In the same way your imagination can be scary, it can also be amazing and fun! So choose the fun!

"Yes!" encouraged Daddy. "And then you can remind your body and mind to feel calm and safe. It is important to feel safe when we are safe!"

Mummy asked, "Wilson, what does it feel like in your body to feel safe?"

Wilson paused to think, then said, "When I feel safe, my tummy doesn't feel wiggly or gurgly. My body feels calm. The sides of my mouth feel happy and I feel good. Then I close my eyes and imagine going to the beach where the sand is pink, the sky is purple, and the water is blue! The sun feels warm on my fur and the breeze smells like freshly baked sugar cookies. I hear the small waves tumbling onto the sand of the shore."

"Good! And what do you remind yourself?" asked Daddy.

Wilson giggled saying, "I remember that I don't have to fight invisible dragons. And I remind my body and mind that it is okay to feel safe when it is safe!"

### Did you know?

It is possible for all of us to have a safe space we can go to in our imaginations! Maybe your safe space is like Wilson's, at the colorful beach, or maybe your safe space is in the mountains with pine trees and cool air, or lying in bed with a soft blanket, or on a tree swing in the middle of the park. It can be anywhere, and you could be doing anything! Aren't imaginations incredible?

with that, Wilson yawned a huge wombat yawn and Mummy and Daddy
wombat smooched him on each cheek. They walked out of his cozy little room
and whispered, "We love you, Wilson."

## Did you know?

You may have a mom and a dad at home,
or one or the other. Maybe you're living
with people who are not your family, or
perhaps you live with your grandparents.
You may have brothers and sisters, or
both, or neither! Whatever your family
looks like can be as different as can be,
but what matters most is that you are
safe. And you can feel safe when you
are safe, even if you have to remind
your body.

As they waddled down the hall to their bedroom, Wilson imagined he could hear the sound of the ocean. Then he took a big breath in through his nose, sighed sleepily, and fell fast asleep.

Here are some truths for you:

You are dearly loved!

You are cherished!

You are smart!

You are brave!

You have a marvelous imagination that will get bigger and stronger as you exercise it.

So now, imagine where you will go in your sleep tonight...

Blue-tongued skinks are shy and calm lizards that live in Australia, Tasmania and New Zealand. These animals eat bugs and plants. When they get scared, they open their mouth, stick out their bright blue tongue, hiss and puff their body up to scare animals away. In the wild, bright colors often indicate venom, but the skink is not venomous—their tongue is just a disguise. They are 12-16 inches long and have fat bodies and short legs.

Echidnas are hatched from eggs and they are one of only two egg-laying mammals! Baby echidnas are called "puggles" and they hatch in only 10 days, then as marsupials, live in their mum's pouch for 6-8 weeks. They often live with their mums in their den for up to one year. Echidnas have no teeth but very long and sticky tongues that they use to eat worms, ants and insect larvae. They are usually between 12-17 inches long.

Black-footed rock wallabies are small and look similar to a teeny tiny kangaroo! They may be 18" tall and weigh only 10 pounds. Since they sleep during the day and are active at night, they are nocturnal, just like Wilson! Grass, fruits, and small shrubs make up the diet of these little creatures and they eat mostly at twilight and daybreak. They are shy marsupials and their babies are also called joeys.

Fairy penguins are between 13-17 inches tall and also called blue penguins because of their slate blue feathers. They are diurnal which means they are awake during the day and sleep at night, like most humans! They live in burrows with the wombats but sleep at night and swim and hunt for fish during the day. These penguins live near the coastline, just like some families of wombats.

Bilbies are omnivorous creatures that are also nocturnal! Omnivorous means they eat both plants and insects. They do not need to drink water, because they get all the moisture they need from the plants and other foods they eat! Bilbies are marsupials and carry their joeys for 3-4 months. They have long ears like rabbits and big black bushy tails with white tips. They are part of the bandicoot family and are wonderful diggers!

Koalas actually live in trees, but they are curious explorers, so that's how they end up at the Wombat Bed and Breakfast sometimes! They are marsupials that mostly live in trees and eat eucalyptus leaves. Eucalyptus is actually toxic, so joeys eat their mom's poop called "pap" so their stomachs can have the bacteria needed to digest the leaves. Koalas sleep 20 hours per day to slow down their metabolism to help conserve energy.

Horned dung beetles are funny creatures that look like real-life unicorns! They have one horn (like a rhino) and wings as well (okay so they aren't actual official unicorns, but isn't it fun to imagine?!). Dung beetles are one of the strongest insects: they are able to carry 1,141 times their own body weight! Dung is another word for poop and they are called dung beetles because they roll dung into balls with their hind legs to live in and to eat! Ew!

Wombats are our favorites! We can't forget to include the hosts of the Wombat Bed & Breakfast! You have learned all about them throughout this book. One final fact for you is that wombats are pretty round and stout, but don't let that fool you. They can run as fast as nearly 25 miles per hour! That is about the speed of an Olympic sprinter!

When kids (and grown-ups) are anxious or have other kinds of big feelings, it is important to acknowledge their feelings and then give them problem-solving coping skills. The "what-if-worry" list and the "what-is-truth" list help them do those very things.

The reason we talk about the stomach feeling "wiggly and gurgly" and his mum suggesting going potty or being nervous is that kids often have a difficult time differentiating the feelings in their stomach. They could be tired, hungry or need to use the restroom (potty or poop), be getting sick, or feeling anxious. We need to help give them options for why their stomach feels strange and help them problem solve. Some of the ways kids may show signs of anxiety could be tummy aches, headaches, pulling their hair, asking the same questions about the same worries, scratching/picking their skin, difficulty going to sleep or staying asleep, or panicking when a parent leaves the room.

On many of the pages, you will find different facts about the extraordinary wombat. The facts are interesting, but they are also silly and fun. Laughter is incredibly important to help with big feelings and release some of the anxious energy and it is also a wonderful distraction when used in a healthy way. There is something extra sweet about settling into bed with a content grin on your face.

Everyone needs to remind themselves that it is indeed okay to feel safe when you are safe. Our minds can get caught up in those "what-if-worries" and we need to remind our bodies and minds of what it feels like to be safe.

Amy Orlovich is a Licensed Clinical Professional Counselor and lives in Boise, Idaho in the USA. She has been married to Brian for 28 years and they have three grown (one is nearly grown) children and one son-in-law! Since she was young, Amy has loved learning fun and extraordinary facts about our amazing world and the people and animals living in it. She wanted to incorporate some amazing animals with some of the tools people need to feel peaceful and calm. Amy has a counseling practice called Waters Gone By and she sees clients who have experienced trauma and other kinds of difficult life circumstances. She utilizes EMDR in her practice and you can learn more about her and her practice at watersgoneby.com. For more tips and encouragement, follow on Instagram: @wilsonthewombatbook and @watersgoneby

## About the Illustrators:

James has illustrated over 50 children's books and created characters and illustrations for countless other children's toys and products over the last 16 years. James has been married to Corissa for 15 years. They enjoy animated movies, board games, and hosting friends together.

Denise has been in the illustration field for 15 years and counting. She has a knack for matching the style of the characters James creates and bringing out captivating coloring in the books they work on together. She has 2 children and is always finding creative and magical ways to bring joy into their lives.

James Koenig and Denise Arends have worked together for many years. They originally worked together at a vector artwork company, drawing everything you can think of. They quickly became good friends and enjoyed working together. Since then, James and Denise have grown into a great team, creating spectacular books, comics, and designs together.

You can learn more about them at: www.freelancefridge.com.

Made in the USA
Monee, IL
20 November 2022

18222182R00024